On The Road

Down Girl and Sit

On The Road

by Lucy Nolan

Illustrations by Mike Reed

Marshall Cavendish Children

Marshall Cavendish Corporation
99 White Plains Road
Tarrytown, NY 10591
www.marshallcavendish.us

Library of Congress Cataloging-in-Publication Data
Nolan, Lucy A.
On the road / by Lucy Nolan ; illustrated by Mike Reed.
p. cm. — (Down Girl and Sit)
Summary: A dog who thinks her name is Down Girl goes on a car ride
to the beach, goes camping in the woods, and reluctantly pays a visit
to the vet with her master, Rruff.
ISBN-10 0-7614-5234-6
ISBN-13 978-0-7614-5234-8
[1. Dogs—Fiction. 2. Humorous stories.] I. Reed, Mike, 1951- ill. II. Title.
PZ7.N688On 2005
[Fic]—dc22
2004027511

The text of this book is set in Garamond.
The illustrations were created in Corel Painter 8.

Book design by Adam Mietlowski

Printed in The United States of America

Marshall Cavendish Chapter Book, First edition

5 6

To Ted, who is nice to setters

—L.N.

To Jane, Alex, and Joe

—M.R.

Contents

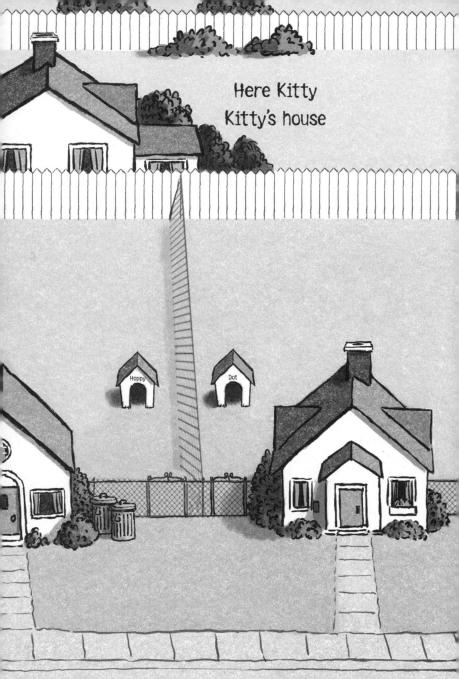

Chapter 1

Fastest Dogs in Town

Hello. My name is Down Girl.

This is my neighbor. Her name is Sit.

We are dogs.

I'm telling you that, in case you might think we are squirrels.

Here's how to tell the difference between dogs and squirrels.

We are smarter.

We are better looking.

And, here's the most important thing. We have cars.

I go all over town in my car. I go with my master, Rruff.

1

Rruff does most of the driving. Okay, Rruff does *all* of the driving.

Whenever he opens the car door, I jump right in and put my paws on the wheel.

"Down, girl!" he says.

"Rruff!" I answer.

"Down, girl," he says again.

Oh, all right. Fine. I let him drive.

At least I'm in the car. You'll never see a squirrel in a car.

Sit and I know all about squirrels. We spend our days chasing them from our yards.

Rruff never chases squirrels. Not even in a car. When Rruff drives, he stays on the road. He doesn't have very much imagination.

Rruff also sits very still. He doesn't know what he's missing. I like to stick my head out the window and lean into the wind. My ears flap behind me in the breeze. I close my eyes and dream that I'm driving.

Sit likes to ride in cars, too. Let me tell you what happened to us last week.

Sit and her master came over. They got into the car with us. Sit's master sat up front. Sit and I sat in the back.

As we rolled out of the driveway, Sit said, "Guess what the squirrels are saying right now."

"Doggone!" I answered. Ha! That is our favorite joke.

We hadn't gone very far when I saw Here Kitty Kitty. Here Kitty Kitty is the cat that lives behind me. I don't like cats. They never stay in their own yards. They are very sneaky and they touch all my stuff.

I leaned into the front seat. I started barking at Here Kitty Kitty.

"Down, girl!"

Rruff elbowed me, and I fell off my seat.

I'm sure it was an accident. I didn't want Rruff to feel bad about it, so I put my paws on the back of his seat. I kissed him.

Rruff slammed on the brakes.

"Down, girl!"

He can call me all he wants, but I'm not going to join him in the front seat. It would be rude to leave Sit.

Rruff sighed and started the car again. For the first time, I noticed the back of his head. His ears aren't very big. They couldn't flap in the breeze, even if he wanted them to! Poor Rruff. I felt so sorry for him, I kissed him again.

This time he swerved.

A car with blue lights pulled up behind us. Its siren was howling. I howled along with it.

The siren stopped. I kept howling, just for fun.

A man walked up to Rruff's window. He said something to Rruff, and Rruff pointed to me. The man leaned down to look in my window.

I kissed him, too.

The man talked to Rruff, and then he walked away. I'm not sure what he said. It was probably something like, "That's a fine looking and very important dog."

That would explain why Rruff put me in the back of the car. That is where he stores all his important things.

I had never ridden in the back before. There wasn't much room to move, and my ears didn't blow in the wind. It wasn't all bad, though. There was a big window and some interesting crumbs.

As we went down the road, I saw all kinds of cool things. Garbage trucks, leaf piles, fire hydrants.

Finally, we got to the end of our trip. It was the beach! Sit and I love the beach. We can relax there. There are no squirrels on the beach.

Rruff and Sit's master unloaded some of the stuff from the back. They left Sit and me in the car while they carried their chairs to the beach. I wasn't worried. I knew Rruff would be back for me.

I knew Rruff loved me. I knew he missed me. And, more importantly, I knew he had packed doughnuts in one of his bags. If he left Sit and me alone for too long, we would find them.

I was too excited to look for them just yet. I crawled into the backseat to wait with Sit.

Suddenly I saw something move by the trash can. It was a cat!

I jumped onto Rruff's seat. I barked. The cat ignored me. That made me mad. I jumped at the windshield and barked again.

I stood in Rruff's seat with my paws

on the wheel. Sit scrambled to join me. Something clicked. Suddenly the car moved.

Rruff raced toward the car.

"Down, girl!" he yelled through the window.

Didn't he see I couldn't stop for him now? The car was rolling. I couldn't believe it. After all this time, I was finally driving. Whee!

Boy, did that cat look surprised! He ran down the hill. We rolled down the hill after him.

"Watch out, cat! We're the fastest dogs in town!"

Uh-oh. The car rolled to a stop. It was stuck in the sand.

Rruff rushed to our side. How sweet! Still, he should have run after the cat. That would have been more helpful. Rruff is not known for his brains.

A crowd gathered around. I knew what they were thinking. They were thinking, "Look at those dogs. They drove that car!"

It's a good thing the crowd was there. Rruff never would have gotten the car out of the sand without them.

Six men pushed the car back up the hill. I hung my head out the window, but my ears didn't go anywhere. The men weren't pushing the car fast enough.

I traded places with Sit. I stuck my head out the window on her side of the car. Nothing.

Oh, well. Not every moment can be packed with excitement.

Besides, I still had the whole afternoon ahead of me. And maybe Rruff would let me drive home.

Chapter 2

Sea Dogs

Rruff opened the doors, and Sit and I jumped out. We stretched our legs and ran to the beach.

I found some old bread. I ate it. I found a smelly fish. I rolled all over it. I found some fish bait. I didn't know whether to roll in it or eat it. I did both.

Next I went to see if Rruff was ready to play. He was sitting in his beach chair. I put my paws on his knees.

Suddenly, I had to shake. I couldn't help it. Water flew everywhere.

"Down, girl!" Rruff shouted.

Well, I'm sorry, Rruff, but it's just one of those things. If a dog doesn't shake, she'll explode.

I didn't want Rruff to be upset with me. So I kissed him.

Rruff wrinkled his nose. I guess he wanted a dead fish to roll in, too. I was about to go find one for him, but he wanted to play in the water.

Rruff dunked me over and over. He was sure to wash the fish smell off me. I didn't say anything. I didn't want to ruin his fun.

Rruff didn't stay in the water very long. Oh well.

I tried to get him out of his chair again, but he wouldn't move. I don't get it. Our masters had all this sand to roll in, but they just wanted to sit.

Sit and I decided to go find someone else to play with. We knew our masters would still be there when we got back.

We found a little girl digging a hole. She wasn't very good at digging. So we helped.

We made the hole bigger and bigger and bigger. Then we stood back and watched. We couldn't wait to see what she was going to bury. Maybe it would be a dead fish. Or a sandwich.

The little girl poured a bucket of water into the hole. That was it. That was all she wanted the hole for. That didn't make a bit of sense.

Our talents were clearly being wasted here. We went to see what was happening over by the rocks. Maybe we could find a smelly fish for our masters.

There were pools around the rocks. Fish were darting around in the water.

"Those fish are awfully small," Sit said.

"Rruff would have a hard time rolling on them," I added.

I wondered what else was in the pools. I stuck my nose under a rock.

A dog should never stick her nose under a rock. I always forget that.

Something grabbed the end of my nose. I don't know what it was, but it hurt.

I shook my head. The thing went flying. It landed on a lady with a hat. She screamed.

I felt bad for the lady. I went to see if she was okay.

But first, I had to shake.

The lady screamed again. Sheesh! She is very jumpy.

Sit and I headed back down the beach. A ball went flying by. I snatched it out of the air.

A group of boys called to me. One of them started running toward me.

Ah! They wanted to play chase.

I ran. I took the ball with me. I knew just where to bury it!

Sit and I rushed back to the big hole. I
dropped the ball in. We kicked dirt all over
it. Then we headed back to our masters.

The boys were shouting. The little girl
was crying. I think they were sad we were

leaving. That's the thing about dogs. People
love us wherever we go.

When we got back to the chairs, our
masters weren't there. We couldn't believe
it. They never move.

We finally saw them swimming in the

waves. We watched them for a while, but decided not to join them.

Some dogs feel the call of the sea, but not us. We felt the call of doughnuts.

Sit and I nosed through our masters' bags. We found the doughnuts. There were only two. Should we eat them?

Hmm. There were two dogs, two masters, and two doughnuts. That sounded about right.

Thank goodness dogs don't know math. That makes all of our decisions easy.

We ate the doughnuts.

As it turned out, two doughnuts were not enough for everyone. We decided not to say anything to our masters.

They knew anyway. When they walked up, they gave us very disappointed looks.

How did they know we ate the doughnuts? Looking back, it might have been because Sit's head was still stuck in the bag.

Our masters sighed and folded up their umbrellas. That meant it was time to go home.

I didn't want Rruff to stay disappointed with me. While he took the chairs back to the car, I looked up and down the beach one last time. I found just what I was looking for! Rruff would be so happy with me.

Rruff came back for his bags and we all walked to the parking lot. Sit and I jumped onto the backseat. It had been a tiring day, but a good day. Sit stretched out and went to sleep, but I didn't. There would be plenty of time for that later.

As the car headed home, I thought about the day and smiled. This was the day that I drove a car! I wanted to remember this day at the beach forever.

Rruff would remember it in a few days, too. That's when he would find the dead fish I packed in his beach bag. He would be so happy.

All the way home, I held my head out the window and let my ears float out in the breeze.

I closed my eyes and dreamed of driving.

Chapter 3

Camp Wild Dog

If I could live anywhere I wanted, I think I would live in my car.

Right now, Rruff and I live in a house. I like our house, but it never goes anywhere. Every morning, I look out the window. I can tell we didn't move during the night.

A car is different. A car can take you far away from the city. I love those days. When I get into the car, I am Down Girl. When I get out of the car, I have become Wild Dog.

The other afternoon, Rruff came home and started loading lots of gear into the car.

That meant we were taking a big trip.

We drove for a long time. We finally stopped in a clearing in the forest.

I jumped from the car and sniffed the wind for danger. I froze.

Rruff froze, too. He looked around to see what I saw.

I didn't see anything at all. I just froze because it scares Rruff every time. Ha! I am just too funny.

There was a creek by the clearing. I ran through the water and rolled in the mud.

I might be in the forest, but I still wanted
to smell my best.

I trotted back to Camp Wild Dog. That
is what I call the clearing where Rruff had
put all of our gear. By this time, Rruff had set
up the tent. He was getting the bed ready.

I jumped on it.

"Down, girl!"

I heard a puff of air, and I slowly sank to
the ground. Did Rruff really expect me to
sleep on this?

The sun was getting lower, and Rruff started building a fire. That meant it was time to eat. Now Wild Dog could hunt for supper.

I saw some hot dogs in a pan. I stalked them. They didn't put up much of a fight.

Those hot dogs were very tasty. I don't know why Rruff didn't bring enough for him to eat, too.

Rruff ate some hot dog buns and looked unhappy. I could have told him that a skimpy meal like that would put him in a bad mood.

When Rruff finished his supper, he played the guitar and began to sing. At least, I think that's what he was doing. He was so out of tune, it was hard to tell. I had to show him how it was done. I got up close to his ear and sang, too.

Rruff elbowed me and laughed. "Down, girl!"

Rruff doesn't like anyone to sound better than him. He needs to get over that.

Rruff put his guitar aside. I'm sure all the animals in the forest were thankful for that. I know I was.

It was getting cloudy and the wind had picked up. Rruff put out the fire. Then he whistled for me and headed down the trail. We were going for an evening walk before the rain came.

This was a chance for Wild Dog to chase squirrels. This is what I was born to do!

Which squirrel should I chase first? They all looked alike. In fact, these wild squirrels looked like city squirrels.

Wait a minute. These could be the squirrels I already chased away from home. I'd have to think about this.

If I had already chased them away from home, why should I chase them again? I might chase them back toward my house.

Oh, this was too confusing.

By that time, it had started to drizzle. Rruff whistled for me to go back to the tent with him, but I wasn't ready.

I saw some tracks I had never seen before. I smelled a scent I had never smelled before. The hair on my back stood up. This was no common city squirrel.

Rruff would just have to head back to camp without me. Wild Dog was on the hunt for real.

I sniffed and walked and listened and sniffed again. I walked around an old log. Then I saw it!

It was the scariest squirrel I have ever seen. It had giant freaky ears and a crazy look in its eyes. What kind of squirrel was this?

It stared at me. I stared back. Then I
saw its teeth. They were huge!

I didn't have a good feeling about this.

I didn't want to take my eyes off the
squirrel, but I had to look up in the trees. I
wanted to make sure there weren't any more
of these creatures waiting to drop on me.

Lightning lit up the forest. The squirrel
twitched its nose.

I ran!

I ran because, uh, I needed to protect Rruff. Yeah, that's why I ran.

The rain was pouring down by the time I got back to Camp Wild Dog. Rruff was in the tent.

The sky lit up again. There was a loud boom. I jumped on Rruff. Rruff jumped up. The tent came down.

We scrambled around. Rruff was shouting. I think he was thrilled that I had come back to protect him.

We crawled out from under the tent and looked for shelter. Guess where we ended up! We ended up in the backseat of the car.

We were safe. We were dry. We were together. It was a dream come true. For one night I got to live in my car!

Even though I slept with one eye open, it was one of the best nights of my life.

When morning came, I was still happy, but Rruff seemed a little upset. Sometime during the night, something had chewed up his candy bar. I think it was that wild squirrel.

Then again, it might have been me.

Chapter 4

The Lady in the White Coat

I love riding in cars, but I am not foolish.

There are times when a dog should never get into a car. A dog should never get into a car when her master tries too hard to get her in there.

It can only end in misery.

Let me tell you what happened this morning.

I was outside chasing Here Kitty Kitty, since he had touched my stuff. Well, I wasn't exactly chasing him, because he wasn't running. He was sitting on the roof of my shed, licking his paws. So I was just running around the shed, doing all my chasing without him. Sit barked from the other side of the fence.

Just then Rruff called me into the house. I could tell he wanted to go somewhere.

"Ha-ha," I told Sit. "Here Kitty Kitty might get into my yard, but he'll never get into my car!"

I ran inside. I couldn't wait to see where Rruff was going to take me.

Rruff was pretending it wasn't important if I went with him or not. That was a bad sign. I ran under the bed.

Rruff tried to talk me out from under there. That didn't work.

Rruff left me alone. He thought I'd forget about it and come out. He sat in the other room and hummed while he read the newspaper.

That didn't work.

Rruff dropped a doughnut near the bed.

He wanted me to think it was an accident. Did he really think I was going to fall for that? Did he really think I'd come out for a doughnut?

I came out for the doughnut.

You never know. It could have been an accident.

Rruff grabbed my collar. He snapped on the leash.

Okay, so he got me out from under the bed. That didn't mean I had to get into the car.

Okay, so Rruff is bigger than I am. Maybe I did have to get into the car.

Rruff talked nicely to me, but I knew where the car was going. We were heading down the scary road. I knew exactly where that road went.

Rruff rolled down my window a little way, but I didn't stick my head out. I was not in the mood.

Rruff pulled up in front of the building. I knew it! This was the house where The Lady in the White Coat lived. There was another person who lived there, too. I don't like to say his name out loud. He lived in The Room.

I decided to escape through the window. It could have worked, too, if the window had been bigger. Instead, I had to wait for Rruff to come unstick my head.

Rruff and I walked into the waiting room. Rruff sat down. I jumped on his lap.

"Down, girl."

I'm sure he meant to hug me, but he accidentally pushed me off. Twice.

There was a terrier next to me. I sniffed him. The terrier sniffed me back. We were having a delightful time. I almost forgot why I was there. I even wagged my tail. I couldn't help it.

Everything was fine until the hall door opened. I dove under the chair and shook, but it was not my turn. It was the terrier's turn.

The terrier's master tugged on his leash. The terrier didn't want to go. He tried to dig in his heels, but The Lady in the White Coat has very slick floors. The terrier slid across the room and through the doorway. It was very embarrassing to watch.

Now Rruff and I were alone. All I could do was stare at the closed door. Rruff tried to talk me into coming out from under the chair. When will he ever learn? That didn't work this morning and it wasn't going to work now.

Suddenly the hall door opened. Rruff lifted the chair and tugged on the leash. I slid across the floor.

I knew I looked silly. I told myself, "Stand up and walk. You can be brave."

Oh, who was I kidding? I slid all the way out of the room and down the hall.

We came to the door of The Room. I shook all over, but we slid on past. Whew!

A door down the hall opened. We slid inside. The Lady in the White Coat was waiting.

Rruff lifted me up and put me on a cold table. I waited for The Lady in the White Coat to yell at him. She never did.

I don't understand. If I so much as put my nose on the table at home, I get yelled at.

I don't know why Rruff likes visiting The Lady in the White Coat. She has no manners.

She looked in my eyes.

She looked in my ears.

She looked at my teeth.

I wonder how she would like it if someone did that to her.

Then she stuck me. I yelped. Yes, I did.

She reached for the cookie jar. Did she think I was going to take a cookie after what she just did to me?

Well, okay. I took the cookie.

She clipped my toenails. It didn't hurt, but I yelped anyway.

She gave me another cookie.

Maybe that's why Rruff comes. Maybe he keeps thinking that one day he'll get a cookie, too. Well, if he wants a cookie, he needs to learn how to yelp.

Finally it was over. There was nothing more to worry about.

Rruff and I went back to the waiting room. There was a German Shepherd. He was shaking.

There was a Saint Bernard. He was hiding under a chair.

There was something in a box making pitiful sounds.

I rolled my eyes. Come on, guys, snap out of it.

Just then, the door behind me opened. The Saint Bernard tried to jump onto his master's lap.

It was embarrassing. All that fuss over The Lady in the White Coat.

But it wasn't her. It was him! It was the Man with the Clippers. He had somehow gotten out of The Room.

He had the terrier—or what was left of the terrier.

I tried to run for the door, but the Saint Bernard was blocking the way. I ran to the corner. I hid behind the box that was making awful sounds. I watched the German Shepherd slowly slide out of the room.

I was sure nothing could ever make me happy again.

I was wrong.

I looked inside the box. Something hissed at me. It was Here Kitty Kitty!

I barked. He scratched my nose. I didn't care.

Today, I had faced danger and lived to tell about it. On top of that, I was free to leave now. Here Kitty Kitty had to stay!

Rruff and I got into our car and drove away. Ha-ha! I have a car! All Here Kitty Kitty has to ride around in is a silly little box. I couldn't wait to tell Sit.

I stuck my head out the window and laughed. A bug flew into my mouth. I didn't mind. In fact, it was kind of tasty.

I watched the road in front of us and wagged. Here's the funny thing about roads. It doesn't matter how scary they are. If you turn your car around and follow them in the other direction, they always take you home.